The Ice Cream BANDIT

To the readers and spoonies who find themselves in books, this one's for you

Crumps Barn Studio
Syde, Cheltenham GL53 9PN
www.crumpsbarnstudio.co.uk

Cover design by Lorna Gray

Typeset in Adobe Garamond Pro

All our books are printed on responsibly sourced paper from managed woodlands and recycled material. Printed in the UK by CMP, Poole.

ISBN 978-1-915067-41-8

The Ice Cream BANDIT

The FIRST FABULOUS adventure for the BISCUIT CLUB

REBECCA McDOWALL

with ILLUSTRATIONS by LORNA GRAY

Crumps Barn Studio

Chapter One

The town hadn't stopped talking about it. The bandit had returned once again. The shopkeepers were cross, but the rest of the town was bubbling with the excitement of the mystery returning to their sleepy seaside home.

Every store that stocked ice cream had been hit and hit hard.

Whoever the bandit was had to have a serious sweet tooth, no small child alone could eat that much ice cream no matter how hard they tried. Strawberry, chocolate, and even the rhubarb flavours had been demolished. This bandit was no fussy eater. This year the mystery robber had returned earlier than usual, the summer holidays were not even in full swing yet, the schools had only just broken up, and the buzzing holidaymakers that flocked there each year had yet to arrive.

The small town's shopkeepers had been caught completely off guard and unprepared.

After overhearing her parents discussing the missing ice cream over their morning coffee, Sophie scrambled around the house. She pulled on her socks while frantically scrawling on a few scraps of paper, not bothering to try and tame her wild locks as she raced to do up her trainers.

With a hurried, "I'll be back for tea, love you," Sophie grabbed her rucksack and hopped out her front door. There was no option of delaying long enough to explain where she could be off to at this time in the morning. This was far too important to wait.

“Hold up!” Her mum called after her. “Have you packed your stick and the phone?” Sophie nodded as she jumped on her orange bike, her trusty helmet squishing her already rebelling hair. “Remember to use your stick if you need to sweetheart. The phone is for emergencies and photos only.”

“Don’t worry Mum!” Sophie called over her shoulder. She tingled with excitement as she raced towards Elijah’s house.

Her rather muddy backpack was empty except for her folded walking stick and the four carefully folded palm-sized scraps of paper.

There had been no time for trying to print anything fancy, Sophie had decided as she eavesdropped on her parents' conversation. Instead, she had hurriedly drawn a single rectangular biscuit on each folded piece.

Her friends would know what to do.

It was the Biscuit Club calling card. An elusive club dedicated to solving the town's mysteries and searching for the next adventure. Once opened, each member would hurry down to the Milkshake Shack on the beachfront. Hiding in plain sight was the smartest place for a secret club after all.

Sophie cycled as fast as she could to each house. Three quick and loud knocks before she shoved each calling card haphazardly through the door, then she was off again as fast as her legs could peddle. There would be no waiting to check if anyone picked up the card. She could smell adventure waiting, and she was going to make sure this was the year that the Ice Cream Bandit was finally unmasked.

Chapter Two

Alex arrived at the Milkshake Shack shortly after Sophie. He slid onto the bench opposite her with a stifled yawn, Oreo milkshake in hand. His striking red hair was windswept from the downhill cycle, undoubtedly taken at breakneck speed. Sophie put her finger to her lips and pointed to the booth behind where they were sitting.

Her notepad and sparkling pink pen were in her hands as she jotted down everything she could overhear.

“I don’t know how it got in. By the time I heard the alarms going off it had cleared me out. Cleared me out do you hear? Only left the bubble-gum flavour, and even then it still didn’t leave enough to sell for one day let alone a season.”

Wallace, the elderly plump owner of Wallace & Sons Sandcastle Emporium had been the first one to be hit this year.

He had his phone to his ear as he added clearly, “I saw it, you know. The bandit.” He paused dramatically. “It’s not a person, lad. A humongous glittering fish, except it was as large as my car yet as swift and quiet as a mouse.”

Sophie heard Wallace sigh loudly, clearly frustrated at whatever response he was getting.

Then he said hotly, "No I haven't hit my head. The cheek of you!"

Sophie felt an idea beginning to form and started scribbling notes frantically in her pocketbook. She never went anywhere without the glittering rainbow notepad. It was stuffed full of mystery possibilities and directions to wherever the next adventure might lie.

Just as she finished her notes, Maisie and Elijah slid into the booth. Both were gulping down their milkshakes, the glint of excitement sparkling about them.

“I heard it didn’t just hit Mr Wallace last night, but three other stores as well!” Elijah blurted out unable to contain his excitement any longer.

“No one’s got a clue. Isn’t this perfect?!” He hastily swallowed a giant mouthful of milkshake as Alex shot him a glare. Perfect for the group but not for the owners of the raided shops who relied on ice cream as part of their summer trade.

Mr Wallace glanced at the overly exuberant group as he waddled grumpily past their table.

He paused momentarily before huffing and turning to them, red faced still from his heated phone call. Maisie was sure the vein above his left eye was throbbing angrily.

"I tell you what kids. You find me a clue, any clue that helps me solve my Ice Cream Problem and you four can have free ice cream for the rest of the summer. Heck, the rest of your lives if it means I get some answers. I know how much you love that mint chocolate chip cone."

He nodded and walked off not waiting for them to accept. He knew they would. The town had been terrorised for six years, and the police still didn't have the foggiest about who the culprit was. When Mr Wallace had given the police his description this morning they had gently suggested he needed a lie down and to see a doctor. Some people needed to know when to believe in the impossible.

Chapter Three

Abandoning their half-drunk milkshakes, The Biscuit Club raced off gleefully on their bikes. They were chuckling loudly as they brainstormed what could be plaguing their town. What, not who – they all agreed it couldn't be human. Mr Wallace wasn't the type to embellish after all, and the seaside town's police force was normally right on the nail with putting a stop to this sort of thing. It was the exact mystery that the foursome lived for.

They leaned their colourful collection of bikes on the stone wall that ran parallel to Danny's Daring Dodgems. From the state of the outside of the ticket office it was clear that it hadn't faired any better than Wallace & Sons Sandcastle Emporium.

Maisie whipped out a small phone and started snapping pictures of the slippery mess that covered the tracks and brickwork while Alex and Elijah snuck round the back to look for more clues.

The four soon felt just as stumped as the adults. There was no clue left, inside or out. Just complete chaos. Helmets had been scattered all over the place, chocolate flakes were melting on the till. No one knew where to start. How could someone leave such devastation in their wake and not a single clue, not one footprint? It seemed completely impossible.

Charles, one of the shop's employees, stood in the doorway, hands in his pockets staring in mystified amusement at the four of them.

"I told Danny while we were checking the dodgems over, that you four would be up here sooner rather than later. First thing that made him laugh this morning. Told me I didn't know what I was talking about." Charles let out a barking laugh. "Surprised it took you four this long to decide to get on the case, it's right up your street."

He indicated to the havoc that lay around them before dropping his voice to a stage whisper. "Have you heard that Danny caught a glimpse of the intruder?!"

The four members of The Biscuit Club felt their jaws drop at this news. Two sightings in one night. The bandit was making mistakes.

Charles smiled. “That’s right. I heard him talking to the police this morning. He kept trying to tell them it was a monster. A huge monster almost as big as the store with hypnotising blue and silver scales – looked like living water apparently.”

Charles paused for dramatic effect, enjoying his captivated audience.

"But if you ask me I agree with the police. The old boss probably saw something he didn't understand and is in shock. But living water? Nah." Charles walked back into the store to start the clean-up.

Sophie listened closely, quietly sketching each description in her pocket notebook. She bit the end of the rubber. Clearly it wasn't a human, nor a bat or a bird, or a dog. But a fish seemed impossible.

Chapter Four

They stopped at Freddy's Desserts next. His once-colourful door had been decorated with picture after picture of the treats they loved, but now it lay in splinters on the floor. Sophie unfolded her walking stick. There was no way she wanted to risk slipping in all the ice cream! The four members of The Biscuit Club tentatively walked around what was left of the front door before freezing to the spot in shock.

There in front of them was Freddy's famed Ice Cream Throne. Except what had once been the coldest, yet most delicious throne in existence was now a small wooden and extremely sticky chair that looked as if it had been cleaved in two.

MA
YOU
OWN
CROWN

It had been emptied completely, except for a lick.

Freddy Senior had stuck a note in the window, they would be closed for the rest of the day while he built another throne.

"It ate my throne, Robert!" Freddy bellowed into the phone. "Its tongue scooped out every dollop until the chair snapped down the middle, don't try to fob me off telling me this was some kid. Pretty sure I've never seen a child with a forked tongue in these parts of town."

The Biscuit Club hid in the shadows listening intently whilst Sophie hurriedly jotted down Freddy Senior's rant. Maisie whispered each clue into her friend's ear while the boys watched awestruck as she sketched out yet another image of their suspected bandit. She chewed the end of her rubber. It wasn't a human, nor a bat or a bird, and definitely not a dog.

Alex motioned for them all to creep closer around him so they could see from his viewpoint. With a shaking finger he pointed toward the back of the eaten throne. As clear as daylight for all to see were two huge clawed footprints in the sticky ice cream that ran all over the tilled floor.

Maisie, with all the grace of a ballerina, whipped out her phone and silently slipped over to the footprint to take a close photo.

"Should have known you four would be sneaking around." Freddy appeared behind The Biscuit Club, mop and bucket in hand, causing Maisie to yelp in surprise and almost drop the phone. "Charles let me know you lot were snooping around but I didn't think you'd sneak in here without asking first." Disappointment and fatigue were clear in his tone.

Alex, Sophie, Elijah and Maisie hung their heads "We're sorry sir. We weren't trying to cause problems, we just wanted to help find a clue to make a break in this case."

"Just run along kids. You mean well, but I got a shop to clean up and a throne to rebuild."

He marched them out of the shop muttering to himself.

There in Sophie's notebook staring back at them was a giant fish, a long forked tongue poking out its puckered lips and two giant claws instead of fins. The Biscuit Club had to agree that even they could see why the police had been laughing at such a description.

Chapter Five

The four members of The Biscuit Club sat on the beach, talking over what they had learned.

“All I can think of is that whatever is doing this, isn’t fussy. I mean rhubarb flavour? Really?” Elijah quipped as he shoved a sandy digestive into his mouth.

“Those claw marks were insane though, they’re bigger than my dog.”

Alex nodded in agreement. “Not ever seen a fish with claws down at the pet shop though, have you?!”

The group snickered but still they stared at Sophie's drawing that lay on the beach between the four of them. Ridiculous it may be but yet none of them could quite shake the feeling that that they were finally on the right track.

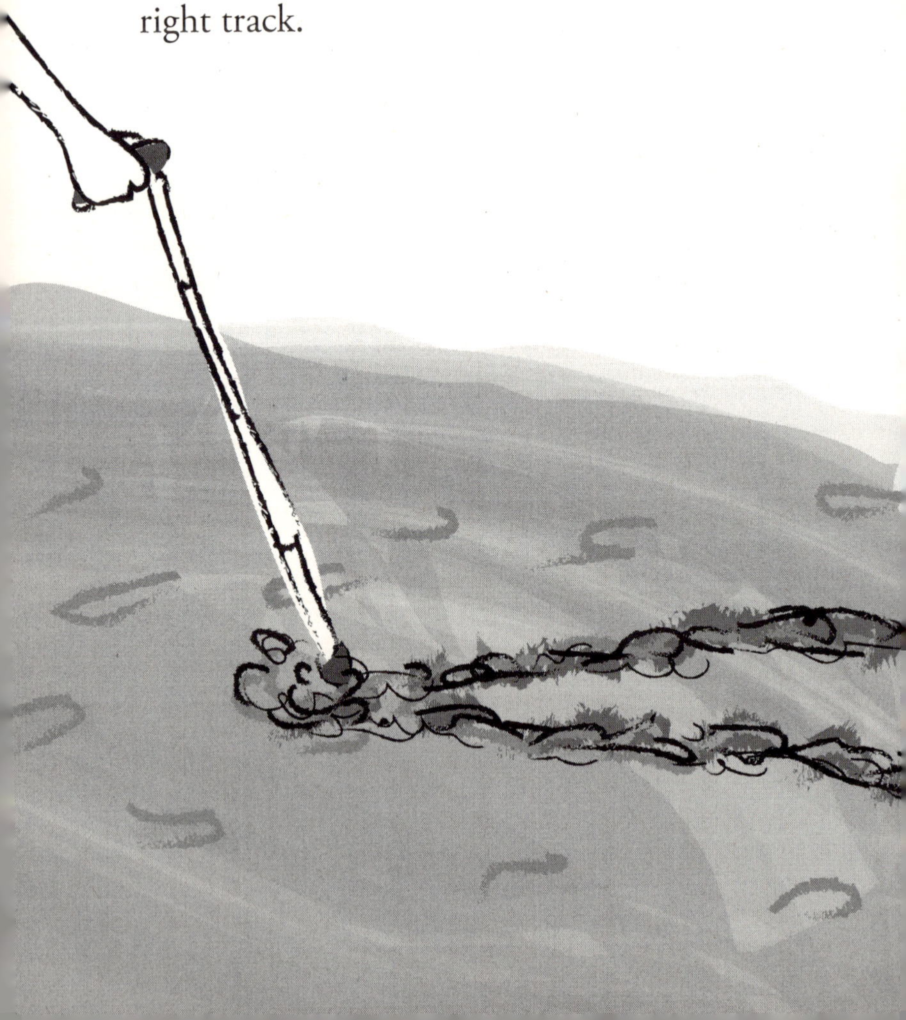

“So we’re in agreement then?” Sophie broke the silence. “The adults are once again completely clueless. There’s no way it’s a human or even a pet. None of us have ever seen a dog with claws big enough to leave those marks and something like a bat or a lizard wouldn’t have a hope of eating all that ice cream, never minding managing to break in in the first place.”

Maisie and the boys nodded, murmuring softly in agreement.

“So that leaves me to think there can only be one possibility left …”

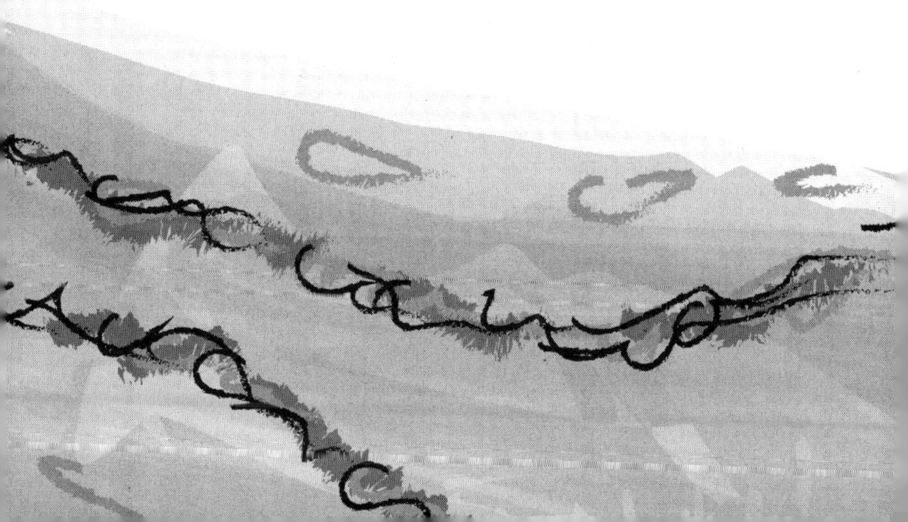

"Our bandit is a dragon …"

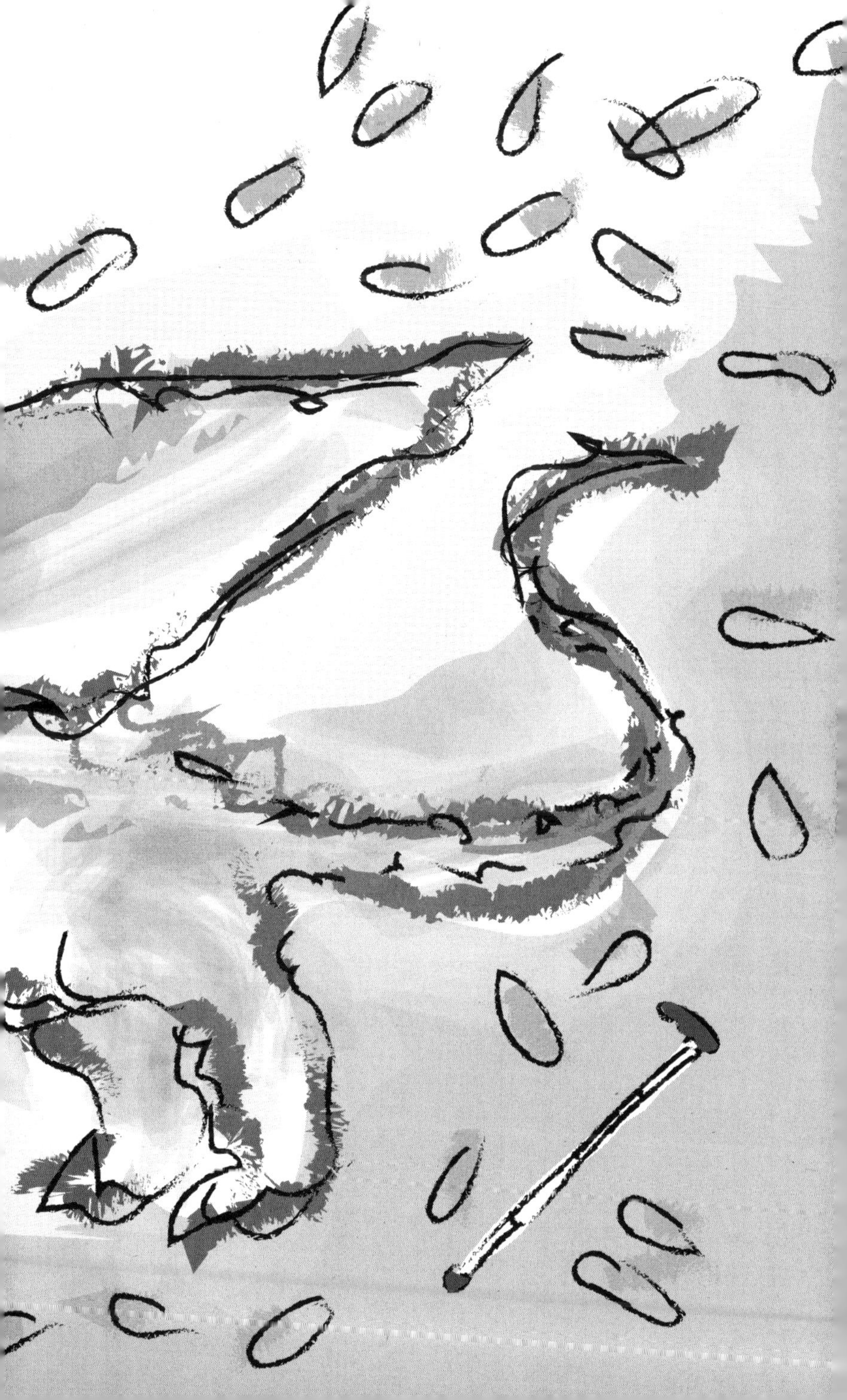

She stopped talking, aware of just how ridiculous her words were. Yet no one argued with her. The boys raised an eyebrow but didn't utter a word. Clearly they were all thinking along the same lines.

"So how do we catch it?" she mused out loud.

"I may have an idea." A disgruntled voice called out from behind them. There was Mr Wallace, his crocs in hand as he made his way across the sand. His ice cream splattered trousers were rolled up to the knees.

"This dragon's a greedy one and there's only one way to catch these things. With a good old fashioned trap."

The children glanced to the plastic bag that spiralled from his fingertips.

"How do you know how to catch a dragon Mr Wallace?" Maisie asked politely unable to take her eyes off the supermarket bag out of curiosity.

His red sweaty face broke into a mischievous smile. "I'm mighty glad you asked." He upturned the plastic bag and shook it hard causing container after container to fall out. "Our little monster loves ice cream, so why not give it what it wants?"

Alex popped open the container nearest him, running a finger along the little soppy substance that was left inside before giving it a tentative lick. He grimaced in disgust.

"Rhubarb. Why is it always rhubarb?" He gulped down what was left of his water trying to get rid of the sickly-sweet taste that clung to his tongue.

Mr Wallace chuckled. “We’ll lure the culprit out and with any luck the bandit won’t be bothering us anymore.”

The Biscuit Club jumped to their feet excitedly, gathering up an armful of containers each. They started to place the plastic tubs along the beach a few intervals away from each other right up to the mouth of Hunter’s Cove.

“We can keep watch for the bandit from in here,” Alex stated as he excitedly rubbed his hands. “Maisie get that camera out, you’re not going to want to miss the shot!”

The club’s excitement was palpable in the air as they stared out at the lure they had created and started their watch.

Chapter Six

The cool of the evening was starting to draw in and The Biscuit Club gazed out at the nearing tide. Their excitement was beginning to turn to anxiety as the group wondered whether the bandit was going to make an appearance.

The four children huddled together whispering quietly about how much longer they should wait before calling it a night and heading home. Elijah's stomach had been grumbling loudly for the last hour and he'd been suggestively counting down the minutes until teatime. Sophie leaned heavily on her stick, her joints protesting from a day spent chasing clues.

"Look!" Mr Wallace's whisper echoed in the small cave, one puffy finger shaking with nerves as he pointed out to the slowly rolling in ocean.

The Biscuit Club squinted out into the darkening sky, looking for whatever Mr Wallace had spotted upon the horizon.

There under the full moon rose the bandit from the night's lazy waves. Its tongue hung out of the corner of its mouth as it rose up into the sky, shaking the ocean drops from its shimmering wings.

"Living ocean indeed!" Sophie gasped, breaking the spell that had rendered them all into silence.

The dragon was easily the size of Maisie's living room as it flew over the pier heading directly towards their carefully laid out trap.

It sniffed the first container once before what sounded like a deep spluttering laugh erupted from it.

"I can smell you children." The dragon spoke with a slow almost musical lilt. "Why have you eaten my ice cream?"

Maisie snapped away with her camera determined to capture enough images to put any naysayers in their place. A dragon. A real life ice cream obsessed dragon.

"WE didn't eat the ice cream." Elijah called back, stalking out the cave. "You ate OUR town's entire ice cream supply. This is just us returning the packing to you to clean up." His words sounded a lot braver than he was feeling. He was sure if Sophie glanced his way she would notice just how much he was shaking.

"My name is Itheriel, but you can call me Icy." The dragon purred as it padded across the cool sand towards the cove.

"Well Icy. I have a few questions for you. As do so many of the other shopkeepers here. Why do you keep eating all our ice cream? Surely there are plenty of big factories you could rob instead!" Mr Wallace had seemingly regained some of his own fire.

"I think what Mr Wallace means Icy, is that we would love to be your friend, and I'm sure the rest of the town would come to love you too. But you can't keep stealing all the ice cream. It's driving away the holidaymakers and, well, we would like to enjoy it too."

The dragon gazed down at the odd little group.

"Friends?" Icy dragged out the word as if tasting it on her tongue. "Perhaps … I come here because the water gets too hot. You are not far from my watery home. The creamy treat cools me down enough to sleep in the summer waters."

Alex and Maisie's eyes sparkled with a thrill as they whispered to each other, before Maisie finally elbowed Alex forwards gesturing for him to speak.

"Sophie's right, I'm sure everyone would welcome you if you stopped raiding the ice cream. Maybe we can work together?" He paused for a deep breath, not quite believing he was really talking to the humongous dragon sat before him. Icy's scales were shimmering with a blue and pearly gleam in the early moonlight.

"Maybe you could work with the town. Come out in the daytime, shelter in this cove from the heat if you need to. A dragon would definitely bring all the holidaymakers back to town and I'm sure everyone would be happy to give you a gigantic helping of ice cream everyday in return?"

Icy looked at the four children and the bumbling man before her. The children's faces shone with excitement. The dragon's purr could be heard the length of the beach, its sugar filled dreams had come true at last.

Chapter Seven

The Biscuit Club raced back to the beach the next morning, dragging bleary-eyed parents in tow. Not one of the parents had believed their thrilling tale of the sugar loving dragon upon their return home last night. The foursome had expected as much, they could barely believe themselves that the bandit was an ocean dweller.

"Come on, faster, I want you to see Icy before the rest of town arrives." Elijah pulled his mum's hand, determined to show her the mythical beast.

"Oh my goodness me." Beverley stopped in her tracks, her hand tightening around her steaming thermos.

There at the edge of the cove lay Icy, the sun bouncing off her colourful scales. Icy grinned lazily at them, before lifting a hypnotising wing to reveal two giant cooler units full of delicious cool ice cream.

The Biscuit Club's mystery had finally been solved. What adventure would be waiting for them next?

THE END

ABOUT THE AUTHOR

REBECCA McDOWALL was born in Hertfordshire and grew up in the small market town of Tring. Here her love of reading was nurtured despite dyslexic challenges. Her other works for young readers include *Cheeky Dragons, Staying Inside With the Cheeky Dragons*, and *A Monster Tea at the Palace* which was awarded the Golden Wizard Book Prize in 2023. Rebecca lives with dystonia and she has previously won the *Visibility Award* for shedding light on invisible illnesses and advocating for awareness. Rebecca is married and lives with her husband in Merseyside with their two mini bookworms and a small library worth of books.

ABOUT THE ILLUSTRATOR

LORNA GRAY was born in Bedfordshire and grew up in the small town of Flitwick. She has always been an artist and particularly loves drawing animals and their friends. She has illustrated many children's books and anthologies for grown-ups. She now lives in the Cotswolds with her husband, three dogs, three horses and two goats.